P9-BJB-459

I Can Read!™

SHARED
My
First
READING

Chicken Said, "Cluck!"

by Judyann Ackerman Grant
pictures by Sue Truesdell

HarperCollins*Publishers*

Chicken Said, "Cluck!" Text copyright © 2008 by Judyann Ackerman Grant Illustrations copyright © 2008 by Sue Truesdell All rights reserved. Printed in the United States of America. No part of this book may be used or reproduced in any manner whatsoever without written permission except in the case of brief quotations embodied in critical articles and reviews. For information address HarperCollins Children's Books, a division of HarperCollins Publishers, 1350 Avenue of the Americas, New York, NY 10019. www.icanread.com

Library of Congress Cataloging-in-Publication Data is available.
ISBN 978-0-06-028723-8 (trade bdg.) — ISBN 978-0-06-028724-5 (lib. bdg.)
1 2 3 4 5 6 7 8 9 10 ❖ First Edition

To R.V.A., my Mom,
who instilled in me a love of reading
—J.A.G.

For Anne
—S.T.

"I will grow a pumpkin,"
said Earl.

"I will grow two pumpkins,"
said Pearl.
Chicken scratched the dirt.

"Shoo!" said Earl.

"Shoo! Shoo!" said Pearl.

"Cluck! Cluck! Cluck!"
said Chicken.

Earl dug the garden.

Pearl planted the seeds.

Chicken scratched the dirt.

"Shoo!" said Earl.

"Shoo! Shoo!" said Pearl.
"Cluck! Cluck! Cluck!"
said Chicken.

Earl watered the seeds.

Pearl pulled the weeds.

Chicken scratched the dirt.
"Shoo!" said Earl.

"Shoo! Shoo!" said Pearl.

"Cluck! Cluck! Cluck!"
said Chicken.

Earl's pumpkin grew.

Pearl's pumpkins grew.

Chicken scratched the dirt.

"Shoo!" said Earl.

"Shoo! Shoo!" said Pearl.

"Cluck! Cluck! Cluck!"
said Chicken.

Then one day

grasshoppers came.

Jump! In the garden.

Nibble.

Jump! On the pumpkins.

Nibble. Nibble.

Jump! Jump! Jump!

Nibble. Nibble. Nibble.

"Shoo!" said Earl.

"Shoo! Shoo!" said Pearl.

The grasshoppers stayed.

Chicken said, "Cluck!"
One grasshopper jumped.

Chicken said,
"Cluck! Cluck!"
Two grasshoppers jumped.

24

Chicken said,
"Cluck! Cluck! Cluck!"
Jump! Jump! Jump!

27

"Hooray!" said Earl.

"Hooray! Hooray!" said Pearl.

"Cluck! Cluck! Cluck!"
said Chicken.

Earl gave Chicken
one pumpkin.

Pearl gave Chicken
two pumpkins.

Chicken scratched the dirt.